A NOTE TO PARENTS

Reading is one of the most important gifts we can give our children. How can you help your child to become interested in reading? By reading aloud!

My First Games Readers make excellent read-alouds and are the very first books your child will be able to read by him/herself. Based on the games children know and love, the goals of these books include helping your child:

- **learn sight words**
- **understand that print corresponds to speech**
- **understand that words are read from left to right and top to bottom**

Here are some tips on how to read together and how to enjoy the fun activities in the back of these books:

Reading Together

- Set aside a special time each day to read to your child. Encourage your child to comment on the story or pictures or predict what might happen next.
- After reading the book, you might wish to start lists of words that begin with a specific letter (such as the first letter of your child's name) or words your child would like to learn.
- Ask your child to read these books on his/her own. Have your child read to you while you are preparing dinner or driving to the grocery store.

Reading Activities

- The activities listed in the back of this book are designed to use and expand what children know through reading and writing. You may choose to do one activity a night, following each reading of the book.
- Keep the activities gamelike and don't forget to praise your child's efforts!

Whatever you do, have fun with this book as you pass along the joy of reading to your child. It's a gift that will last a lifetime!

Wiley Blevins, Reading Specialist
Ed.M. Harvard University

ISBN 0-439-26464-2

12 11 10 9 8 7 6 5 4 3 2 1   1 2 3 4 5 6/0

Illustrated by Jim Talbot
Designed by Peter Koblish

Printed in the U.S.A.
First Scholastic printing, April 2001

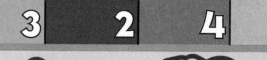

Don't Wake Daddy

Late-Night Snack

by Jackie Glassman • Illustrated by Jim Talbot

SCHOLASTIC INC.

New York   Toronto   London   Auckland   Sydney   Mexico City   New Delhi   Hong Kong

Good night, kids.

Good night, Daddy!

I'm hungry!

Me, too! Let's go.

Shhh! Don't wake Daddy.

Let's go.

Shhh! Don't wake Daddy.

We are almost there!

Where are the girls?

They went to get cake! Let's go.

Yikes! The radio!

Shhh! Don't wake Daddy.

Squeak! Squeak!

Shhh! Don't wake Daddy!

Where is the cake?

Daddy! Who woke you up?

Yum! This cake is delicious.

Bedtime Buddies

In this story, the children sleep with dolls, stuffed animals, and blankies. Do you have a bedtime buddy? On a separate sheet of paper, draw a picture of yourself sleeping with your favorite buddy.

R Is For . . .
Which of these begins with *R*?

Noisy! Noisy!

In the story, the kids make lots of noise on their way to the kitchen. Do you remember which noise is first? Which is last? Number each noise below in the same order.

A Midnight Snack

Everyone loves a midnight snack! Circle your favorite midnight snack. Then, on a separate sheet of paper, draw another midnight treat, and write a poem or story about it.

Clock Match

The kids in the story have a digital clock and Daddy has a clock with hands. Match the clocks in column A to the clocks showing the same time in column B.

A   **B**

Rhyme Lines
In each line, name the pictures to make a rhyme.

I see a _____ on the _____ .

I see a _____ on the _____ .

I see a _____ near the _____ .

The Big Sleepover

Imagine you are sleeping over at the kids' house in the story. Write a letter to a friend describing what it is like. Be sure to include the part about the midnight snack. Draw a picture, too.

New Endings

In the story, Daddy shares his cake with the kids and everyone is happy. How else could this story have ended? Look at the pictures below and then retell the story with each of those endings. Then draw and tell an ending that you make up.

Answers

Clock Match

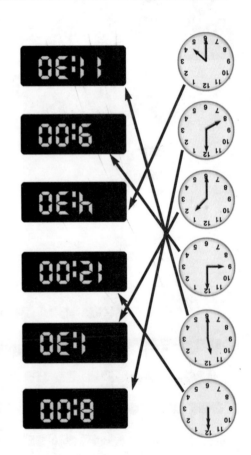

Rhyme Lines

I see a SOCK on the CLOCK.

I see a DUCK on the TRUCK.

I see a SNAKE near the CAKE.

Noisy! Noisy!

The order is roller skate, dog, radio, and rubber ducky.

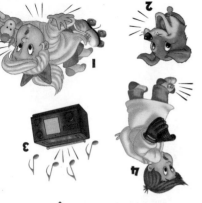

R Is For . . .

These begin with R:

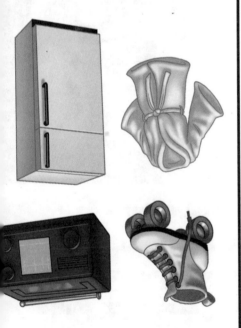